The Best Halloween Hunt Ever

by John Speirs

Cartwheel
·B·O·O·K·S·®

SCHOLASTIC INC.

New York Toronto London Auckland Sydney Mexico City New Delhi Hong Kong Buenos Aires

To Siggy, Tilly, Rolly, Alexandra, and John

ISBN-13: 978-0-545-06867-3   ISBN-10: 0-545-06867-3

10 9 8   13 14 15/0

Printed in the U.S.A.   40
This edition first printing, August 2008

How to Use This Book

The children are going to spend Halloween with Alexis and John's grandparents in the country. There will be friends to meet, lots of trick-or-treating, and a big Halloween party. You can enjoy the fun, too! Follow the rebuses and look for all the hidden treats in the colorful pictures. Watch out for the tricks! Don't get too lost in the mazes and look out for the batty bats throughout the book.

John   Sara   Tina   Alexis   Roy

The answers to all the puzzles are on pages 26-32.

In the schoolroom, before Halloween arrives, the children make tricks, treats, and Halloween decorations to surprise their teacher.

John has hidden

Sara has hidden

Tina has hidden

Alexis has hidden

Roy has hidden

How many batty bats do you see?

Tina's father collects the children to drive them to the country.

John sees

Sara sees

Tina sees

Alexis sees

Roy sees

The batty bats are here. How many do you see?

They stop at a farm to pick pumpkins for jack-o'-lanterns.

John picks

Sara picks

Tina picks

Alexis picks

Roy picks

Find your way through the maze to the biggest pumpkin.

Grandma has hidden treats and tricks all around the house to welcome the children.

John finds

Sara finds

Tina finds

Alexis finds

Roy finds

Can you find the batty bats as well?

The garden is being decorated for the party, but already the children are searching for treats.

John finds

Sara finds

Tina finds

Alexis finds

Roy finds

It's getting dark and the batty bats are everywhere. How many can you find?

All along the road, trick-or-treating is in full swing.

John finds

Sara finds

Tina finds

Alexis finds

Roy finds

Don't forget to look for the batty bats!

The schoolyard has been turned into a Monster Maze, with tricks and treats all around.

John finds

Sara finds

Tina finds

Alexis finds

Roy finds

Can you find these five friends, too?

Inside the Haunted House,

John sees

Sara sees

Tina sees

Alexis sees

Roy sees

Are their friends there? Can you find the batty bats, too?

The children and their friends visit the Halloween Fair where there are lots of surprises.

John sees

Sara sees

Tina sees

Alexis sees

Roy sees

Can you find the batty bats?

As the children and their friends run home, they pass the Halloween Parade.

John sees

Sara sees

Tina sees

Alexis sees

Roy sees

How many batty bats can you count flitting through the crowd?

Home again in time for the Halloween party!

John finds

Sara finds

Tina finds

Alexis finds

Roy finds

The batty bats have joined the party, too. How many can you find?

Answers

pages 4-5

In the schoolroom, before Halloween arrives, the children make tricks, treats, and Halloween decorations to surprise their teacher.

John has hidden

Sara has hidden

Tina has hidden

Alexis has hidden

Roy has hidden

How many batty bats do you see?

pages 6-7

Tina's father collects the children to drive them to the country.

John sees

Sara sees

Tina sees

Alexis sees

Roy sees

The batty bats are here. How many do you see?

Answers

pages 8-9

pages 10-11

Answers

pages 12-13

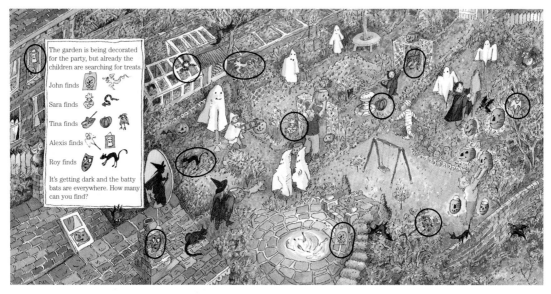

pages 14-15

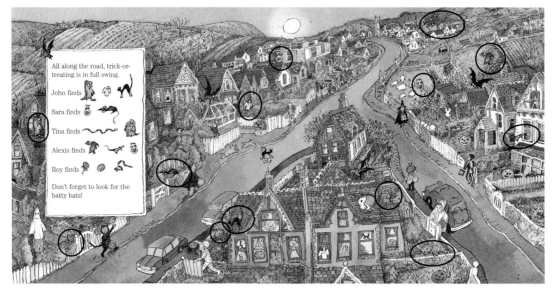

Answers

pages 16-17

The schoolyard has been turned into a Monster Maze, with tricks and treats all around.

John finds

Sara finds

Tina finds

Alexis finds

Roy finds

Can you find these five friends, too?

pages 18-19

Inside the Haunted House,

John sees

Sara sees

Tina sees

Alexis sees

Roy sees

Are their friends there? Can you find the batty bats, too?

Answers

pages 20-21

pages 22-23

Answers

pages 24-25

Batty bats are in each scene.

There are three in the schoolroom.

There are three in the city.

There are four at the farm.

There are four at Grandma's house.

There are five in Grandma's garden.

There are four along the road.

There are four in the schoolyard
Monster Maze.

There are three inside the Haunted
House.

There are six at the Halloween Fair.

There are five at the Halloween
Parade.

There are five at the Halloween party.